Harriet Maxwell Converse

The Ho-De-No-Sau-Nee the Confederacy of the Iroquois the Six Nations

A poem bound with Birch Bark legends of Niagara founded on traditions

among the Iroquois, or six nations

Harriet Maxwell Converse

The Ho-De-No-Sau-Nee the Confederacy of the Iroquois the Six Nations
A poem bound with Birch Bark legends of Niagara founded on traditions among the Iroquois, or six nations

ISBN/EAN: 9783337175467

Printed in Europe, USA, Canada, Australia, Japan

Cover: Foto ©Andreas Hilbeck / pixelio.de

More available books at **www.hansebooks.com**

THE
HO-DE'-NO-SAU-NEE

THE CONFEDERACY

OF THE

IROQUOIS

[THE SIX NATIONS]

A POEM

BY

HARRIET MAXWELL CONVERSE

NEW YORK & LONDON
G. P. PUTNAM'S SONS
The Knickerbocker Press
1884

Press of
G. P. Putnam's Sons
New York

THE
HO-DE'-NO-SAU-NEE.

THE CONFEDERACY OF THE IRIQUOIS.

[THE SIX NATIONS.]

" Ah ! it grieves my heart when I look around and
see the situation of my people, in old times united
and powerful, now divided and feeble. I feel
sorry for my nation ! When I am gone to the
other world, when the Great Spirit calls me away,
who can take my place among my people ! Many
years have I guided the Nation ! "

[From the appeal made by Red Jacket (Sa-go-ye-wa-tha) to
the Council of the Six Nations, after having been deposed as
ruler and Chief of the Senecas, to which honor he was right-
fully restored.]

> Sa-go-ye-wa-tha, sage and warrior,
> Legislator and commander,
> In the harmony of freedom
> From no vulgar race descended;

Noble was thy grave demeanor,
Great in action, wise in council !
By thy ancient rights of honor,
Unto fear thou wert a foeman !
Regal in thy passion's vengeance,
When with hostile fury burning,
Orator and fearless warrior,
In the sternest mould of Nature
Thou wert in thy birthright monarch
Of thy glorious battle scars !

———

Stoic, in humiliation
In thy fortitude exalted,
With thy soul apart communing.
Merciful was thy compassion.
In thy heart, all life's emotions
Gracious were by touch of pity,
Chastened were by love fraternal.
When in tenderness deploring
All the sorrows of thy people !

———

Logan, Brandt, and Shenandoah
Were the kin-folk of thy forests ;
Mohawks and the On-on-da-gas,
Senecas and the Oneidas,
Cayugas and the Tus-ca-ro-ras !
Bold and brave and valiant hunters
Chiefs and Orators and Sachems—
Loyal keepers of the faith—
Of the race who smoked the peace-pipe
By thy wigwams and thy lodges !

———

Iroquois—with laws unwritten—
Though thy Sachems had no cities,
And no temples thy religion,
Though thy league for secret records
Had in art no pompous structure
Rearing glories to its name ;
Beautiful thy simple fabric,
In its grandeur was inwoven
With the brotherhood of union,

All its covenants made sacred
By the calumet of peace !

———

Beautiful thy humble homage,
For the blesséd benedictions,
Of the changes of the seasons,
In their endless alternations
In thy mid-vales and thy mountains
When the draperies of Spring-time
Wrought the vestments of the Summer
On the pines and oaks inlocking
All the elm trees and the maples !

———

Beautiful were thy thanksgivings
To the Giver of thy harvests,
When, in gratitude of offerings,
In thy frequent rites avowing
All the mercies of His blessing
In thy festivals of planting
To the teeming earth committing,

For its nourishing unfolding,
All the seed growths of thy Autumn !

———

Beautiful thy meditations
In thy consecrated forests,
Fragrant in their odorous incense
When—though groping in the darkness—
Thou wert lifted up and strengthened,
In thy earnest firm endeavor,
Nearer drawn to one Great Spirit
In thy ardor of devotion ;
Wiser than the Greeks or Romans
In the godly inspiration
That the Deity hath given
To all hearts of human kind !

———

In the fullness of his knowledge
Faith sustains the Christian martyr;
Thou, enduring keenest torture,
Worshipping at verdant altars
In the pathos of thy trusting,

In thy natural religion
Nearer were to God's own Presence,
Through thy dim divine monitions,
Listening to the golden whispers
Of the Spirit's voice, revealing
To thy human souls thy God !

———

Iroquois ! departed people !—
Children of our living foliage—
Victims of successful warfare
In the viewless snare of Fate ;
Not in servitude's oppression,
Not by power or subjugation,
Yielded thou thy lakes and rivers
And the rugged untilled borders
Of the confines of thy lands !
By thy haughty spirit fearless
In the domains of thy fathers,
In thy right of tributation,
Thou wert passive in submitting
To the light of peace that blighted,

In its withering embrace,
· All the years of thy duration
In the thraldom and the shackles
Of the boundaries of man !

Iroquois ! thou wasted people !
All thy council fires extinguished,
Waiting not, thy hapless nation
Knoweth not the hope expectant
Of their lights and kindling fires !
In the boundless limitation
Of Time's great eternal shadows
Thy sun behind the hills is rested
In its everlasting west !

And of thy departed pageants
Who unto the distant ages,
And the centuries in waiting,
Will reveal the voiceless record
Of thy warlike expeditions ?
Thy nativity of kindred ?

And thy lonely desolations?
When by Time—in flight enfolded—
Unanswering in its strange mutations,
Thy once noble mighty nation
Hath forever lost its place !

———————

Ah ! belovéd Country,
In thy blesséd land of beauty,
In thy poetry of kindred,
In the beauties of tradition,
May the writers of thy verses
In thy scenes of sylvan pageants
Sing in euphonies of praises
All the legends of this people
In the loftiest of lays !

———————

On thy ever-flowing rivers,
Where their tuneful names are written,
Symphonies, bequeathed in rhythm,
Sing unto thy fertile valleys—
To thy pensive listening valleys—

Enchanted in the lovely lore—
While upon their placid bosoms
Dream the themes of lulling lyrics
In the undertunes of sound !
Courteous elm-trees, and the maples,
Gracious in the rapturous sunlight,
Bending to thy peaceful meadows
Whisper, in their soft vibrations,
Of their generous hunting grounds !

———————

Where their battle-cries resounded,
In the savage repetitions
Of their congregated numbers,
All thy harvests, rich, abundant,
In fruitful plenty crown thy land !
Where the dirges of their death-songs
In the echoes solemn linger,
And thy yielding fields are sunny,
Ploughshares, in their loamy furrows,
In a mournful resurrection

Turn their rusted-headed arrows
To the everlasting skies !

———

'Neath the oaks and solemn pine-trees—
Lithe, and tall, and scarred, and glorious
In their sympathetic shade—
Swift of foot, with council tokens
Signalled by their belts of wampum,
Sped their messengers of warfare
And their summoners of law !
Gone for ever are the forests,
Like their unremembered people,
Lavished in the broadened pathways
Of the whirls of loud confusion !
Silent now the singing bowstring,
Sheathed for ever are its arrows
Quivered in the hush of Time !
In their trails abide thy highways,
In the tumult of thy traffic,
To processions of progression

Opening wide their gates !

When to thee, belovéd country,
And thy blesséd land of beauty,
In the records of recession
History opens wide its pages,
Let thy gracious men of letters,
In the scenes of human conflict,
Reproduce this sorrowed people
In their virtues of affection !
In the pathos of relation,
Tell to future generations
All the valor of the red man
In the language of his nation !
In the symmetry of Mohawk
And its glory of religion
When translated in its grandeur
By its ready worded warrior
The Tha-yeu-da-në-gë-a ! *

---

* Brandt, who translated and published in the Mohawk
tongue, the Gospel of St. Mark, and the Book of Common
Prayer.

In the On-on-da-gas learning
And its fluency of tongue !
In the Senecas high sounding,
And eloquence of speech !
In Oneida's whispering softness
And its harmony of tune !
In the pathos of Cayuga,
In emotions of its vengeance
In the sad retaliation
Of the mourning * Tah-gah-jute !
All were people of our forests !
All were people of our valleys !
In their council fires were kindled—
Paling in their dying—embers
Where dear Liberty was nurtured,
In its first creative breathings,
On our flowery fragrant sod !
In the poetry of Nature,
Mournful are their mute petitions
In the everlasting silence

---

* Logan.

Following fast each passing day !

Will no faithful stone, recording—
In the monumental glory
 Of its pale historic marble—
All the bravery of their birthright,
Lift unto the gaze of ages
All their storied power and honor ?
Will their legends and traditions
Go untuned in songs of nations ?
Or, enshrouded in a darkness,
In their natal earth embosomed,
Will, in sorrow, all this people,
In dim sepulchre unnoted,
Yield their ashes to oblivion
And to silence yield their names ?

$$\frac{sx}{1.00}$$

BIRCH BARK

LEGENDS

OR THE ORIGIN OF THE WOLF TOTEM

BIRCH BARK LEGENDS

OF NIAGARA.

FOUNDED ON TRADITIONS AMONG THE

IROQUOIS, OR SIX NATIONS.

A STORY OF THE LUNAR-BOW;

(Which Brilliantly Adorns Niagara Falls by Moonlight),

OR,

ORIGIN OF THE TOTEM OF THE WOLF.

DEDICATED TO THE MEMORY OF

JOINSTAGA,

FROM WHOM MANY LEGENDS OF THE ALMOST FORGOTTEN PAST WERE OBTAINED
BY THE AUTHOR

OWAHYAH.

Union Printing and Publishing Company's Print. Lockport, N. Y,
1884.

PREFACE.

MY preface will be a few citations from reliable authorities to introduce to my readers the people of whom I write:

GOV. CLINTON, in a discourse delivered before the New York Historical Society, says: " Previous to the occupation of this country by the progenitors of the present race of Indians, it was inhabited by a race of men much more populous and much farther ad. vanced in civilization ; that the confederacy of the Iroquois is a remarkable and peculiar piece of legislation ; that the more we study the Indian history the more we will be impressed with the injustice done them. While writers have truthfully described their deeds of cruelties, why not also quote their deeds of kindness, their integrity, hospitality, love of truth, and, above all, unbroken fidelity?"

WASHINGTON IRVING says: "The current opinion of Indian character is too apt to be formed from the degenerate beings, corrupted and enfeebled by the vice of society, without being benefitted by its civilization. That there are those, and a large class of them that have with moral firmness resisted the temptations, with which they have been surrounded, and command our highest esteem."

VOLNEY, the French Historian, pronounces the Iroquois "The Romans of the West."

W. H. C. HOSMER, "The Warriors of Genesee."

ORSEMUS TURNER, in his History of the Holland Purchase, says. "The existence of the IROQUOIS upon the soil now constituting Western and Middle New York, is distinctly traced back to the Period of the discovery of America.

"Their traditions go beyond that period. They fix upon no definite period in reference to the origin of their confederacy. Their Councils were held along the southern shores of Lake Ontario, and upon the Niagara River, before the first adventurers, the Dutch, and French Jesuits appeared in the valley of the Mohawk; and there are evidences of a long precedent existence that corresponds with their traditions."

And their Council Fires are still kindled though they burn not as brightly as of yore. Nor do the young braves listen to the wisdom, or ever now in their Councils witness the allegorical or figurative language so beautifully illustrating the discourses of Red Jacket, Corn Planter, Farmers Brother and other Chiefs, thus eulogized by PRES. DWIGHT: "In strength and sublimity of their eloquence they may be fairly compared with the Greeks."

The INDIANS say: "We listen to your stories, why do you not listen to ours? Although civilized, you use not the rules of common civility."

OWAHYAH

BIRCH BARK LEGENDS OF NIAGARA.

FOUNDED ON TRADITIONS AMONG THE

IROQUOIS OR SIX NATIONS

Within sound of the thundering cataract's roar once worshipped the roaming sons of the forest in all their primitive freedom. They recognized in its thunder the voice, in its mad waves the wrath, and in its crashing whirlpool the Omnipotence of the Great Spirit— the Manitou of their simple creed.

Also in the rising mist, the flight of the soul, and in the beautiful bow—the brilliant path followed by the spirits of good Indians to their Happy Hunting Ground.

With this belief came the custom of yearly offering a sacrifice to the Great Spirit, or whenever any particular blessing was to be acknowledged, or for some wrong perpetrated, to propitiate the righteous anger of their Deity of the roaring waters.

The sacrifice, or offering, consisted of a boat filled with fruit, flowers and any precious gift, which was to be paddled over the foaming cataract by one either drawn by lot or selected by the chiefs; or, as often happened, a voluntary offering of life, as it manifested heroism beyond their usual test of torture. Martyrs thus sacrificed had this consolation : that their spirits were sure to rise in the mist and follow the bright path above, while bad Indians' spirits passed down in the boiling, crashing current, to be torn and tossed in the whirlpool, there to linger in misery forever.

With all thy present loveliness—smooth paths cut 'round thy rocky banks, covered with trailing vines and bright, soft mosses, nature's beautiful tapestry ; flights of steps, half hidden with gay foliage, displaying at almost every turn majestic scenery ; bridges thrown over the bounding, foaming rapids, from island to island, opening bower after bower with surprises of beauty at every step. Scattered here and there the nut-brown Indian maids and mothers, among the last of the race—still lingering around their fathers' places and working at the gay embroidery—soon to pass away forever.

Yes, with all thy loveliness, the circle of mirth and gaiety, reflecting happy faces of thy present worshippers, tame is the scene compared with the traditions of a by-gone race, which, notwithstanding the simplicity in forms of customs that governed them, were among the brightest pictures of American life—always associated with the beautiful forest, which together are passing away, and oblivion's veil fast gathering around them.

Thy rocks, now echoing the gay laugh of idlers, first rang with the wild war-whoop, or sent back the Indian's low, mellow songs of peace, or mingled with the heavy roar of thy falling waters the mournful dirge of the doomed one, to the Great Manitou.

STORY OF THE LUNAR BOW,

(Which brilliantly adorns Niagara Falls by moonlight),

————OR————

Origin of the *Totem of the Wolf.

FIRST LEGEND.

The tradition of the Lunar Bow, the Manitou's bright path, or the origin of the totem of the wolf, was traced with a scene long remembered at their councils, passing from generation to generation, and still sung by the Indian mothers in their far-off home towards the setting sun——the last foot-hold of the dark sons of the forest on this their native land. On the east side of the Falls of Niagara, before the hallowed waters of the mist fell on the pale-faced warrior or the sound of the axe had even broken the great stillness of their undisputed soil, the dark shadows of the primeval forest fell only on rock and wigwam.

The red-topped sumach and sweet sassafras grew thick on either side, while ledges of rocks here and there pierced the foliage of the cedar-crowned banks, 'round which tumbled and roared the mad waves, leaping like frightened does in wild confusion to their final plunge. The narrow Indian trails, winding around swamps, over hills, and through ravines, were the only paths that led to this their Great Manitou.

*The coat of arms of a clan.

The drowsy sultriness of an American summer pervaded this secluded spot, harmonizing with the unceasing roar of the Great Falls. Ever and anon, tall, dark forms might be seen suddenly appearing from the thick foliage of the underbrush, through which their paths with difficulty wound, and silently their painted faces and gayly plumed heads dropped 'round the big wigwam. Important questions waited the decision of their wisest Sachems, and runners had been sent with wampum to call together distant Chiefs, who, with braves and warriors, as became the dignity of the wampum, answered by their presence quickly and in silence.

Near the brink of the Falls, beneath an aged pine, reclined a well-guarded, sorrowful, but haughty band. Their fine symmetry, noble height, and free carriage, were especially attractive. They were all young warriors, whose white paint presented emblems of peace : their plumes were from the beautiful white crane of the sunny forest, which designated the southern land from whence they came.

A gleam of pride flashed across their dark faces, while their attitudes bespoke both defiance and despair. A tall, stately looking youth appeared to command from these few the deference due a Chief. He was leaning against the old tree, looking for the first time on the great sheet of falling waters, where soon himself and followers would probably end their tortures by a welcome leap. Their noble bearing had

GREAT OAK.

attracted the eye of the Sachem's daughter, the Gentle
Fawn ; she, with a few young Indian girls, half hid
among the whortleberry bushes growing luxuriantly
around the smaller wigwams of the camp, were dividing their attention between the stately captives and
weaving the gaudy wampums to be bestowed, with the
shy little weavers themselves, upon such young braves
as should be deemed worthy by the great council.
Their stolen glances of admiration and pity, however,
were intercepted by the young brave who brought
home and so suspiciously guarded the prisoners. He
was a fierce, wicked savage, with repulsive, glistening
eyes, evincing a cunning, revengeful disposition.

At the side of this savage hung a string of fresh
scalps, and a gleam of exultation shot across his
swarthy visage as he pointed to the gory trophies at
his belt, saying :

"The Black Snake s scalps are fresh from his enemies, the fingers of the Gentle Fawn cannot number
them."

"The Fawn does not like the smell of blood,"
quickly answered the sensitive maid. "The Black
Snake is a boy, and does not know his friends from his
enemies."

"The Fawn has been taking lessons from the mock-
ing-birds," replied Black Snake. "and has learned
many tunes ; she sings now for the ears of the sunny
Eagle, whose wings are too feeble to fly. His last
flight will be short (pointing to the cataract) ; he will

not need his wings, and the Gentle Fawn will soon learn to sing to Black Snake. The Fawn is an infant, and Black Snake will feed her on birds' eggs. Approaching with a noiseless step, he continued, in a lower tone : " The Black Snake will be a great warrior ; he must build a lodge of his own whereon to hang his enemies' scalps (shaking them in her face), and the Gentle Fawn will light his pipe."

· With a suppressed cry the Fawn sprung to her feet. In an instant from the long wild grass at her side appeared a huge wolf, of unusual size and strength, which the powerful creature owed in a measure to the affectionate care of its mistress. She had found it when young, reared and fed it with her own hands, and they had become inseparable friends and protectors to each other.

With an angry growl and flashing eyes the wolf warned the Indian back. Black Snake pointed his flint-headed spear with a look of disdain at the heart of the watchful beast. His arm was suddenly arrested by the hand of the Sachem, Great Oa

" Does the Black Snake make war with the women ? Wouldst kill my daughter's four-footed friend ? Has the young brave only arrow-heads for his friends ? He must go back to his mother's wigwam : let her teach him how to use them."

The dark frown passed from the Great Oak's face as he addressed his daughter. With a watchful tender-

ness seldom found in the breast of a warrior, the stern
old Sagamore's voice grew soft as a woman's.

" My daughter will follow her father ; he knows not
his wigwam when the Fawn and her four-footed friend
are not there."

Thus saying they immediately left the discomfited
brave. In passing by the stranger captives, a sigh escaped the old Indian as he saw the sympathetic looks
t'i t passed between them and his daughter, and com-
par; l that noble young Chief, so soon to pass away,
wi.h th: treacherous warrior who aspired to fill the
War Chief's place, and receive his daughter with the
ti'le. The War Chief was slain on that same expedi-
tion that conquered and brought home the prisoners.
Another was to be chosen and the captives disposed of,
which was the business that had called together Chiefs
from distant places. Occupied with sad thoughts, that
brought him no comfort, he was attracted by the low
whine of the wolf, and upon turning discovered him
fondling around the captive Chief, who seemed equally
pleased with him ; at the same time he caught the ill-
omened look of Black Snake, distorting his face with
rage, jealousy and revenge, as it glowed from beneath
his tawdry plume of many colors. Hastening his
daughter along, who was quickly followed by the wolf
as she gave a peculiar call, they passed silently out of
sight.

As the dark shadows of night gathered closely
around, made brilliant by innumerable fire-flies, sport-

ively decking all nature in spangles, women and children disappeared to their wigwams, while their dusky
protectors seated themselves 'round the great fire, the
red flashes of which fell brightly on the strongly bound
prisoners, proud and defiant, awaiting their doom.

Only one more night and the mild rays of the moon
would fall on good and bad alike—would gaze on the
beautiful, bright colored path over the dark and fear-
ful abyss they were so soon to follow to the Happy
Hunting Ground. The breaking of the waves against
the rocks on the shore, the melancholy cry of the night
bird, like soft music, partially subdued their tortured
spirits, and each recalled with fond longing the memory of a distant home now lying in ashes, and the
sound of some voice now silent, whose tones would go
with them to the Manitou's home.

Calm night, our soothing mother, bringing rest to
all, freed them at last from the insulting taunts of
their savage guards as their swarthy forms were swal-
lowed up in the surrounding darkness.

Oh! how many heartfelt and anxious prayers have
been sent, Niagara, to rise on thy light mist to realms
above.

The Indian's simple supplication, so full of hope and
faith, needed not the assistance of other creeds to be
heard by *his* Great Manitou. And if thou dost pray
sincerely for strength, Grey Eagle, unflinchingly to
stand thy torture and joyfully to take thy final leap,
it will be given thee.

As the dampness of night fled from before the rays of the morning sun it revealed a cooler, calmer crowd around the big wigwam.

In sight of the great waters, and almost deafened by its thundering, warning voice, Sachems, Chiefs and Warriors were quietly and orderly assembled. Directly in front were placed the securely bound prisoners, surrounded by aspiring young braves, too willing to show their skill in throwing arrows and tomahawks as near as possible to the captives' heads, delighting the dusky children, who with the women formed the outside circle.

For several minutes the pipe, with the sweet-scented kinny-kinick, was passed from one to another in silence. Not a word escaped them, the Chiefs vieing with each other in betraying no symptom of idle curiosity or impatience. At length a Chief turned his eyes slowly towards the old Sachem, and in a low voice, with great delicacy in excluding all inquisitiveness, addressed him :

"Our father sent us the wampum ; we are here, when our father speaks his childrens' ears are open,"— again resuming the pipe with due and becoming solemnity.

After a moment's silence, during which the children even became mute, the Sachem arose with dignity and commenced his brief story in a solemn, serious manner, becoming himself and the occasion.

"'Tis well ; my childrens' ears shall drink no lies.

Their brothers have been on the war-path. The Great
Manitou smiled on the young brave; sent him back
with fresh trophies and prisoners; not one escaped.
The Great Manitou has also frowned on his people,
hushed their song of triumph, sent them back to their
tribe crying, 'where is the great War Chief, the nation's pride?' Do my sons see or hear the War Eagle
in the wigwam of his people? No; he came not back;
the Manitou needed him; he has gone to the Happy
Hunting Ground; our eyes are dim; we shall see him
no more. Who will lead the young braves on the war-
path? Who will protect the wigwams, the women,
children, and old men? Let my children speak, their
father will listen."

With the last words all excitement seemed to pass
from him, and the face of Great Oak assumed that im-
movable expression which rendered it so impossible to
surmise what really were his thoughts or wishes. The
murmuring wails of the women in remembrance of
War Eagle and the threatening tomahawks that were
shaken at the prisoners, all ceased as slowly the first
Chief again rose to speak.

"Let our brother, the young brave who followed
where War Eagle led, and returned with prisoners and
trophies to appease his mourning people—let the Black
Snake speak, that we may know how to counsel our
father."

The eyes of the young warrior thus alluded to
flashed with fierce delight—his nostrils dilated with

BLACK SNAKE.

strong emotion. Passing with a haughty stride in front of the Chiefs, displaying to all the bloody trophies at his side, without dignity or feeling, but in an excited, vindictive manner, he gave an exaggerated account of the foe and the battle ; spoke of the loss of the War Eagle ; called on the young braves to help revenge his death, swinging his tomahawk around the heads of the prisoners, counting the scalps he had torn from the heads of their people, forcing them in their faces with malignant pleasure, and calling them women, who would cry when their tortures commenced. He said he only waited to attend the joyful dance before going on the war-path to avenge more fully the death of their Chief and earn the right to have a wigwam. He howled his fierce demands for an opportunity to show his willingness to execute the sentence the Chiefs should pass upon the prisoners. Then, adroitly pleading his youth, he said he would not ask to lead the braves on the war-path—he would follow where some braver one would lead. Throwing the string of scalps among the crowd, he said the women might have them to hang on their lodges—he was too young to carry them. Feeling he had made sufficient impression of his bravery to leave the decision in the hands of the Chiefs, without noticing his triumph in the applauding multitude, his fiery eyes rolled proudly from Chief to Chief. He passed with a haughty step before the Sachem, who had several times rather depreciated his bravery, rejoicing in this public opportunity of boasting a little before the Chiefs, evidently thinking it would greatly contribute to his ambitious purposes and make a good impression on the Sachem's dark-eyed daughter.

As he finished his speech the crowd commenced reciting the virtues of their deceased Chief, calling for revenge, and insulting the prisoners with every epithet their wild imagination could suggest. A dissatisfied "hugh" from the old Sachem caused the first Chief again to rise, when in an instant all again became quiet, such were the peculiar customs of these people and the great influence of their Chiefs and Rulers. In a calm voice he addressed again the old Sachem:

"Thy son has spoken with a brave and cunning tongue; yet he speaks not to the heart of his Chief. He is ready to strike the enemy. Who carries more arrows or sharper ones than Black Snake? Whose stone-headed war club is deadlier? Whose tomahawk is freer on the battle-field? The Black Snake coils himself under the bushes and springs upon his sleeping enemy. When they would strike him he is gone, and their club falls where he once stood. He will be a great warrior when he gathers a few more years. He needs experience to lead the young braves. Let our father speak from his heart, that he may hide nothing from his children, then will they know how to counsel."

Thus called upon, the old Chief rose with a calm brow, and advancing with great dignity, slowly scanned the faces of his dusky audience. His eyes beamed with respectful, hopeful submission on his circle of Chiefs, also upon the women judges, who make the final decision in choosing a new Chief after hearing the arguments in favor of each candidate. Glancing towards Black Snake with a stern, unwavering countenance, regarding the priscners with unaffected sympathy, and finally resting with a fond look of painful solicitude upon his daughter, who was seated on a mossy carpet beneath a large tree, within hearing distance of all that was said—the wolf, the Fawn's devoted friend, coiled at her feet, and her neglected wampum carelessly thrown over his glossy neck—in a clear, low voice, as one who having once determined upon the necessity no hesitating fears should prevent, Great Oak addressed the now watchful and silent multitude.

"It is true the feet of the young brave have been far away on the war-path ; his tomahawk and arrows have not been idle ; he crept like a serpent upon his victims ; his war club was stained with their blood ; their scalps were many by his side ; he came not back empty-handed ; he brought prisoners to his people and gifts to his Manitou."

The low murmur of applause now increased to a shrill howl, which the echoing rocks sent flying on, mingling with the roar of the falling waters. This approval being taken for their approbation, which promised support to his opinion, Great Oak, thus confirmed in his remarks, continued :

"War Eagle came not back to his people; his wig-

wam is lonely ; did he fly away like a frightened bird
at the sight of his enemy?" An angry "hugh" was
uttered sympathetically. "Did he die with his body
filled with the arrows of his enemy?" After a short
pause he answered himself :

"No, my children, the tomahawk was buried in the
back of his head. Was his foe behind him? Yes, my
children, but not Grey Eagle and his brave little band
now standing in front of you. They were also in front
of War Eagle, but he saw in them no enemies ; Grey
Eagle saw no enemies then. Look at the paint of
Grey Eagle and his braves ; do you see the red and
black worn by a Chief on the war-path? Has the
Manitou thrown a cloud over the eyes of your Sachem ?
I see only the white paint of peace and friendship.
When were our fathers ever known to bind a friend ?

"Your Sachem has lived too long ; he has lived to
see the ceremonies of his people laughed at by boys—
the sons of his friends with friendly colors bound at
his feet by his own children, and the tomahawks of his
people ready to bury themselves in their flesh."

The deep silence which succeeded these words suffi-
ciently showed the great veneration with which his
people received their ideas from their oldest Chief.
All listened with breathless expectation for what was
to come. Black Snake and his few followers scowled
revengefully, though not daring to reply. The Sachem
continued :

"The Great Oak can no longer overshadow and protect his people—can no longer preserve the ceremonies of his fathers. His strength has gone, and his counsels fall to the ground like the branches of the dying tree ; he is needed here no more. When my children next fill a canoe for the Manitou, place the old tree and all belonging to him in it. The tired birds that have flown to him for rest he can no longer protect, and it is time his people burned him down out of the way, that the saplings may find more room to grow. Let the arrows and tomahawk of Great Oak be prepared for the Manitou—he would pass from his people forever."

With the last words he moved slowly from the circle, and, placing himself by the side of his daughter, closed his eyes, manifesting his resignation of all interest in their present or future state. An appealing wail from the multitude brought several Chiefs to their feet.

"Our father must not leave us; his voice is the voice of wisdom ; when his childrens' ears drink lies and their counsels are foolish the wind brings truth to the ears of Great Oak; they will fade away when Great Oak's shadows are withdrawn. Can his children feast and dance when their father hides his face with shame? The Manitou has counseled the Great Oak in his sleep ; the women are in tears, and the young men are silent. We have spoken, and we wait for the voice of our Sachem."

"Why do my children wait for the voice of a Chief,

whose words fall like leaves in the cold blast to be trod on by boys?"

"The words of the Great Oak, like the leaves, can bury the people. Let our father speak to the hearts of his children that they may know what to do. Has the wind whispered in the ear of our father and he tells not his children their story? We listen for the voice of our Chief."

The old Sachem slowly opened his eyes and once more rose to his feet, standing erect in front of the tree whose name he bore, where still, with the wolf stretched at her feet, the Gentle Fawn remained seated. Without deigning a glance upon the multitude, but looking in the distance, as if invoking unseen aid from the air or sky, dropping their figurative language, he spoke in a low, prophetic tone.

"Yes, there has been whispering in the ears of your Chief. He shut his eyes on all around him, and opened them on a sunny spot, far off, where the rivers know no ice and the moccasin never tracks in the snow. There were more wigwams than he could count, filled with happy people. He saw a band of braves as straight as the pines of their forest go on a long path to get furs and meat for their people. After moons of success they joyfully returned; but not to hear the voice of their fathers or ever to see their faces again. The hand of the foe had spared none; their homes were in ashes; their friends sent without food or presents on their long journey to the Manitou's hunting-ground. I saw these tired, sad hunters gather the scattered bones and relics of their tribe in a large circle, placing plenty of furs and food, with pipes, beads and arrows in the center, and cover them high with stones and earth that wild beasts could not move. And they placed the Manitou's mark on this mound that no foe would dare to desecrate. Then turning their faces from their once happy home they sought a new one, and people to help them revenge this deed and recover their land. Winding their way to the land of snow and ice they saw approaching a band of warriors covered with emblems of peace, and, leaving their stony weapons in care of the younger braves, they walked open-handed to meet the strangers. War Eagle stood foremost among them. While passing the calumet* of friendship their ears were deafened with the war-whoop from many mouths. A tomahawk flew swiftlier and deadlier than an arrow and hid itself in the head of War Eagle."

Then, turning his eyes upon the multitude, he would question, and, looking off in the distance, in the same prophetic voice answer:

"Did the tomahawk fly with the stranger's hand? They came open-handed—left their weapons behind them. Did any of War Eagle's braves protect him while his spirit was passing on its long journey? No; the arms of yonder brave protected him until they were bound to his side. Can War Eagle's spirit leave his friend to

---

* Pipe of peace.

receive the torture of the condemned and be tossed in those dark whirling waters forever? No; I hear his moans mingle threateningly with the roar of the Manitou's voice. His spirit cannot rise to the beautiful path while his friends are prisoners to his people. Would you leave War Eagle forever hovering over the turbulent waters? Who will cut the thongs and set the spirit of War Eagle free by freeing his friends?"

The wild cries of the multitude were stilled by the long protracted howl of Black Snake as he sprung in front of the Chiefs. With a dexterous flourish of his tomahawk he separated the thongs, liberated the prisoners, and with a wave of his hand commanded silence, while, shouting in a loud voice, he replied to the old Sachem :

"Our father asks who bound War Eagle's friends! It was the spirits of darkness that blinded his childrens' eyes to the color of Grey Eagle, and whispered in their ears, 'they are enemies.' It was the spirit of darkness that killed War Eagle and whispered in the ears of his braves, 'revenge his death.' It is the voice of the good Manitou that whispered to the Great Oak, and he has saved his children from the Manitou's wrath and freed the spirit of War Eagle."

This ingenious speech showed the cunning of some candidates for office even in those early times, and had the desired effect of winning the confidence of many of his dusky auditors. Long talks followed within the circle by the Chiefs, while preparations were being

made for feast and dance around the council fire that
night.

Aye, Niagara! thou didst lull with thy awful and solemn voice as anxious and also as happy hearts beneath
the soft furs that wrapped those dusky maidens—
mingling their sweet voices with thy deep bass, dancing beneath the old trees on thy wild banks—as any
there have been since in the princely halls where the
old trees once stood, beneath silks and diamonds, that
rival thy beautiful drops, to music that drowns for a
time thine own tremendous voice.

The attention of the Chiefs being directed to Grey
Eagle, the youthful Chief stepped lightly but proudly
in front of them. His manner plainly indicated him a
brave warrior and hunter. As he spoke of his people,
now nearly exterminated, he pointed out to the council the necessity, and expressed his willingness, of
merging their existence in that of another tribe. Many
looked upon him with sympathy and regard. Speaking of the foes of his people, his dark eyes lighted up
with contemplated revenge—his mouth curled with
contempt. He called them snakes with forked
tongues; he wished to drive them from the ever green
and pleasant valley of his fathers; he wished to share
the land with his brothers of the snowy hills. He
proved his skill as an orator by swaying the minds of
his hearers, and amidst great rejoicing stepped back to
the side of his own braves.

The old Sachem looked at him encouragingly, while

the shy Fawn, gathering up her no longer neglected
wampum, bounded away to mingle with the Indian
maidens, followed by the devoted wolf, and the affectionate eyes of her father and of many admiring
braves.

The feast and dance continued long into the night ;
but sunrise found the warriors and braves straightening
their arrows and sharpening their stony points and
newly cording with sinews their idle bows, withing
the heads of their tomahawks, war-clubs and spears.
Great and earnest preparations were made to follow
the river in its noisy course past its dark whirling ba-
sin, down the stony mountain to where it mingles its
wild dancing waves with the calm and beautiful lake,
bringing only the faintest murmurs of the great falling
waters to their favorite hunting grounds.

Within that valley, before the sun drops beneath
the bright waves of Ontario, will be decided by indi-
vidual skill, unassisted by friendly influence, the right
between Black Snake and his adopted brother, Grey
Eagle, to fill the place made vacant by the death of
War Eagle.

This was the decision of the women. Among the
Indians genealogy is reckoned on the mother's side
alone ; and, therefore, the important business of select-
ing a candidate to fill the place of War Eagle, who
left no near relative, devolved upon the women, who decided the successful combatant was to be the future
War Chief of the tribe and claim the wampum with
the old Sachem's dark-eyed daughter.

Sympathy was pictured in most of the faces of those dark warriors, when passing the Great Oak's wigwam they beheld the moist eyes and tender leave-taking of that heroic old Chief and his motherless child, whose future depended so much on the coming contest, as following one after another they disappeared in the forest.

"The Gentle Fawn will stay in the shadow of her wigwam and work on her wampum." And the old Chief, whose words were law, also disappeared, following the narrow winding path, watched by the Fawn till the dense foliage hid him from her view. Without hearing the slightest noise the Fawn felt a hand upon her shoulder. Turning quickly, she beheld the pleasant face of Grey Eagle. Turning his hand in formal recognition, he addressed her :

"The Grey Eagle's eyes are very true, and his arms are very strong; shall he shut his eyes when he draws his bow ? "

"May Grey Eagle's aim never be truer or his arm stronger than to-day." And love-light flashed from the soft eyes of the pretty Seneca maid.

"The Fawn has spoken well ; Grey Eagle hears. When the wish-ton-wish sings his evening song Grey Eagle will be here again. The Fawn will welcome him."

The last of the warriors disappeared, followed by the old women and children, the latter with shouts and songs, going far towards the brow of the mountain, where evening would still find most of them gathering sticks and pine cones to light the evening fires.

About seven miles from the great cataract, towards the north, when following the river, is seen the famous Queenston Heights. where the force of waters has cut through solid rocks to a depth of about three hundred feet, and it is equaled in grandeur only by the cataract itself. This deep chasm in winding from the falls forms the great whirlpool—the terror of the poor aboriginals. From the brow of the mountain the most gorgeous landscape bursts upon the view.

A splendid picture, with the broad waters of Lake Ontario, forms a magnificent background. The mountain sides are broken by deep ravines and huge precipices rising to a great height. The scenery is wild beyond description. On the highest elevation of this rocky cliff, on the western shore, stands the Pillar of Brock, like a giant, guarding the borders of the Queen's Dominion.

Under the eye, at the foot of the mountain, nestles the pretty village of Lewiston. The banks of the river are lower and less rugged, and here commence the beautiful flats that reach to the shore of Ontario. The lake from this elevation is seen like a miniature ocean, spreading far and wide until clouds and water blend. On the left, the foaming, dashing river, passing furiously through the rocky gorge, here becomes quiet, winding its peaceful way through woods and meadows, its soft liquid blue dividing the Dominion from the

United States, and gradually widening until its waters mingle with Ontario. There, standing opposite and frowning upon each other, are the forts Niagara and Massussauga, where successively have contended French, English and Americans. Four villages appear within this view, on either side of the river, with their tall church spires, from which sweet, melancholy notes come floating on the air, tranquilizing the senses with the beautiful scene, interspersed by meadows and grain fields, thickly dotted with cottages, surrounded and half hidden among orchards and lovely gardens, diselosing hundreds of happy homes; while from this elevation deep repose gives softness to the whole picture. The same beautiful river and lake and rock-bound mountain surrounded the Indian's favorite hunting-ground; but a dense forest, divided by marshy creeks, protected their game and sheltered themselves.

Thus secluded, hundreds of wild songsters filled the air with music, while the melancholy notes of the wish-ton-wish's evening song traditionally had power to sooth their savage natures. This sweet, pensive scenery, decked with summer's lovely green or autumn's wampum dyes, with morning's glittering dews or evening's fire-flies' transient gleams, illuminating the darkest places; the distant murmur of the waterfall, the sympathetic cooing of the wild ducks, the cedar-scented air, all tended to thrill the Indian bosom with sensations not less melancholy, not less pleasing, than the present unsurpassed and magnificent view charms all beholders.

Seldom so many warriors met at one time on these quiet flats, and never contested champions more earnestly than did Black Snake and Grey Eagle on that day for the two prizes in one; never were spectators more enthusiastic. Their triumphant whoops echoed along the river banks and their joyous applause animated the fatigued warriors, while side combatants of various ages fought their mimic battles, blending the whole in a scene of wild excitement and confusion. Grey Eagle was an expert archer, but he had found his equal; hence the conflict was so long, and had, from its even tenor, become so engrossing. One instant's hesitation would probably decide the contest with critics so quick to perceive with both eye and ear the least deviation from their standard customs. After passing successively through the exercise of war-clubs, spears and tomahawks, to the bow and arrow was left the decision. Again preparing for the contest after their own fashion, omitting no caution or form, the combatants brought all their warrior skill into requisition. Challenge after challenge was given and taken with equal confidence. The impression on the warrior spectators was exciting; admiration of such unexampled dexterity gradually increased, finally swelling into sounds that denoted lively opposition in sentiment, when suddenly, with an ominous flourish of his bow, as it fell at the feet of Great Oak, Black Snake with a single bound stood in front of the Chiefs. This unexpected movement produced attention and silence while he spoke:

GREY EAGLE.

"Black Snake sends a true arrow, but the Manitou guided Grey Eagle's. The Manitou whispered truths in the ear of Great Oak and defeated the evil spirit. The Manitou says to War Eagle: 'I send a warrior to your people to fill your place, and Grey Eagle, the chosen of the Manitou, will be a great warrior.'"

All of Black Snake's former pride and exultation seemed supplanted by humility. Not the least demonstration of jealousy or revenge was to be traced in his artful face, while he continued :

"Grey Eagle will lead the young braves on the warpath. Let our father send an offering to the Manitou, that he may drive the evil spirit away from Black Snake, and he will be Grey Eagle's brother and fight by his side. Black Snake's arrows are true, and the cries of our enemies will fill the forest, while every squaw can deck her lodge with scalps."

With an appealing glance at the circle of Chiefs, Black Snake modestly retired and they held their talk.

According to their customs, captives were either adopted by the captors and enjoyed all of the rights and privileges of the tribe and confederacy, or sentenced to death, attended by all of the horrors of savage torture. If adopted, the nation knew no difference between her own or adopted children. In the former council by the falling waters the Chiefs had concluded to adopt Grey Eagle and his braves; therefore the women had an undisputed right to select him as one of the candidates for War Eagle's successor, which nomination was ratified by the Chiefs. The women being undecided between the rival candidates, left the final decision as before mentioned to skill or chance. It was more through chance than skill that Grey Eagle won, for both were well-drilled, powerful warriors. But he had fairly won the two prizes, and the conclusion the Chiefs came to was this:

Their great Manitou had evidently sent him to them for some wise purpose. A human sacrifice must be made, as had long been their custom, for the Manitou's good gifts and to redeem Black Snake from the power of the evil one, this sacrifice must be made while the moon was the brightest, which was the present time. It was that the bright light might more fully reveal the brilliant path of the just. As those sent as an offering to the Manitou would go direct to the happy home above, freed from all trouble forever, when the selection was once made they would become reconciled, and make themselves believe it a great favor bestowed and cause of rejoicing. The subject for the sacrifice was most frequently selected by lot from a few the Chiefs would name; but this time it was Black Snake's privilege to make the selection and arrangements, as he was next to Grey Eagle as a warrior, and then the sacrificed spirit was especially to atone to the offended Manitou for Black Snake's rashness while under the influence of the evil spirit. At a signal for silence from Great Oak he made known these conclusions, and Black Snake again came forward, and, with a great deal of self-depreciation, expressed his wishes as follows :

" After the calumet with the soothing kinny-kinnick shall refresh each Chief, while its light curling clouds bear their good resolutions on high, let Great Oak and Grey Eagle be first on the backward trail; rising the big stony hill, still keeping the trail, without entering any lodge, the first one their eyes rest upon—be it one of the men, one of the women, or one of the children— will be the one the Manitou wants. Let the Manitou make his own selection ; Black Snake is not worthy."

During the delivery of this speech his swarthy countenance kindled with a satisfied expression well calculated to conceal the dark malicious plans that struggled in his breast. His very nostrils appeared to dilate with hidden exultation.

Hurriedly passing the calumet, soon a light, fragrant cloud from the sweet-scented kinny-kinnick rose on the air like evening incense, making valid and unchangeable each resolve that tribunal of Chiefs had passed.

While they were yet smoking, Black Snake, recovering his bow and arrow, called for some young braves who could track the deer and help carry the venison back to their lodges, as a feast and dance accompanied each council. The chiefs would smoke in the shade until the fiery eye of the Manitou, satisfied with the purposes and promises of His simple-hearted children, would fall asleep beyond the waters of Ontario, where already the last rays were beginning to color clouds

and waves, till lake and sky seemed a bright vision of
the promised land the doomed one must soon enter.

"The hunters will be back here before the wish-ton-
wish sings; if the chiefs are gone the hunters will follow," said Black Snake, as himself and about twenty
dusky boys, flourishing their bows and arrows, leaped
along the skirt of the forest and soon disappeared.
They wound their way towards the east, where the
deer frequented a marshy tract of land, Black Snake
now assuming all the superiority of a chief and leader,
his boasting, haughty manner returning, as he related
what great deeds he could do, and his name would
make his enemies tremble. Having excited sufficient
awe and veneration among those artless Indian boys,
he pointed to fresh tracks, and waving his hand to the
north, said :

"The deer have gone to the clear water to drink ;
the young brave who kills the first deer shall follow in
the steps of Black Snake on the war-path. Black
Snake will go prepare for the feast and dance, and the
evening fire for the great chiefs ; the young braves will
follow with their venison the back trail ; they will not
go before the old chiefs."

This sudden and unexpected announcement was received with a joyous shout by the aspiring young
braves, who, thus stimulated, quickly disappeared,
leaving Black Snake alone.

A hasty glance at the sky showed him the Manitou's
eye had moved but little since he left the chiefs, and

had some ways yet to travel before disappearing for the night, and his satisfied look said, " 'Tis well," for Black Snake had much to do and much to bring about before the fiery eye would again throw his searching rays upon this wild and wayward child of the forest.

A fierce and fixed expression settled on his swarthy features, contradicting all that assumed humility while in the presence of the chiefs.

Following a direct path to the south-west, with his fast Indian lope, crossing the creeks on the well-known beaver bridges, nothing impeded his speed, and in an incredibly short time he found himself on the brow of the great stony-hill, where his path soon struck the river trail, leaving the council of chiefs many miles behind him to the north. He gave a peculiar whoop, composed of a quick succession of notes terminating in a prolonged sound, which made the forest ring till it died away in the distance, silencing terrified bird and squirrel and making the stillness that followed doubly still. Speeding on toward the lodge, as he neared the great water-fall, he again repeated the shrill call; this time faint answers reached him from different directions.

Then a sharp, solitary note, repeated at short intervals, and answered in the same manner, and with the exclamation " Hugh!" in a satisfied tone, the tired warrior seated himself for the first time since morning at the root of a large tree, holding his head in his dark sinewy hands, as if that was more weary even than his over-exercised limbs. Soon there appeared several Indian boys and old women from different sides of the trail. He held a hasty confidential talk with them. That he did not truthfully explain anything, in fact, misrepresented the whole, was only too natural for Black Snake. But in his own way he revealed the final decision, making a double sacrifice of the human offering—both body and soul; he told them their spirits would be given to the evil one and sent to the turbulent waters, there to be whirled forever in sight of the bright path they never could follow.

This story, as calculated, struck terror to the hearts of his awe-stricken hearers, and had the desired effect. Instantly the dense foliage hid their frightened faces as they fled from the river trail, and only the mimic cry of bird or animal, known as a warning of danger to all within hearing, the leaping or plunging through the underbrush was all the eye or ear could detect after Black Snake's communication, which sent the berry pickers and cone gatherers back with the fleetness of the deer to hide themselves in their lodges. Black Snake was again following with his greatest speed the river trail, not pausing till near the Great Oak's lodge, where, assuming the position and actions of the reptile whose name he bore, he crawled to the side of the wigwam, where, unobserved, he watched for a few moments its solitary occupant. Seated on a robe of the soft furs of the beaver, weaving the plaits on her now highly prized wampum, while the prolonged gaze, interrupted with restless flashing from the dark eyes of the

Fawn, bespoke the anxiety with which she had waited the result of that long, long day, which would also decide her fate. Wearied with picturing the future in its brilliant lights and dark shades, as Grey Eagle and Black Snake alternately figured in her thoughts, and wearied with waiting for the song of the evening birds, she is suddenly startled from her meditation as a shadow falls across the lodge, and Black Snake stands before her.

Springing to her feet and spasmodically grasping the wampum, fearing Black Snake had been victorious and had come for his reward, was the impulse of the moment; but the subdued and brotherly manner assumed by Black Snake reassured as he gently addressed her.

"The Grey Eagle is a great chief, and Black Snake is his brother. Grey Eagle looks as he rises on the stony-hill for his wampum, that he may sit in the circle of chiefs. Shall the Swaying Reed meet Grey Eagle with her wampum? Is the Fawn too timid to go? Black Snake will stay with the Fawn and let Swaying Reed fly on the trail towards the stony hill."

"No! No!" exclaimed the Fawn. "The Swaying Reed loves Black Snake; her feet would be slow on the trail to carry the wampum to Grey Eagle. The Fawn will go to meet her father and the tall chief, while Black Snake sings in the ear of Swaying Reed, who is never tired of the voice she loves so much."

"The Fawn has spoken well; but Grey Eagle must take the wampum from the one his eyes rest first upon

as he rises on the stony hill.   The Fawn saw the
Indian women follow the trail towards the great flats,
to gather berries and pine cones; she must shame the
moose in her flight, and hide under the bushes, if she
would see Great Oak, and Grey Eagle first as they
mount the hill.   If the Fawn would fill the pipe and
kindle the fire for Grey Eagle in his own wigwam, let
him not know she is near until she stands before him.
I have said."

"The Fawn's ears have been open; her feet will not
be slow; she will follow the hidden path, until she
reaches the great rocks of the hill.   The Fawn will do
as her brother tells her.   The Swaying Reed is waiting
for Black Snake."

And ere the day songsters had finished their sweet
melody, or the *wish-ton-wish had yet commenced its
evening song, the half frightened Indian maid had hid
herself near the summit of the hill, under foliage so
dense, she felt not the fast falling dew, as breathless
she waited the coming steps.   From her safe hiding
place she saw the white plume of Grey Eagle waving
over his happy, excited face, as with his light elastic
step he appeared first; erect and tall like the cedars
around him.   Next came her father whose wrinkled
countenance, softened with paternal care and watch-
fulness, had long lost the fierceness and native fire of
his youth, followed closely by his chiefs.   He passed
slowly along the trail, hardly daring to raise his eyes,

---

*Whippoorwill.

it being the death warrant to whomsoever they should fall upon. Suddenly the bushes parted and the Fawn bounded into her father's arms. To accurately describe the agony of this scene would be impossible ; constern-ation for a moment held them spell-bound ; horror was pictured in faces so long trained to conceal the work-ings of the mind, and for the first time the Fawn remained uncaressed in her father's arms. Astonished and grieved she turned to Grey Eagle ; the light had fled from his face, and his soul apparently ; he seemed petrified and lifeless as the rock he stood upon. Even the poor wolf, missing his usual attention, or from some inexplicable cause, commenced to howl pitifully as he leaped from one to another.

The spell was broken by a young chief not old enough yet to feel the responsibility of the customs of his fathers, from which life nor death would tempt an older chief to deviate, hopefully exclaiming :

" It was the wolf the Sagamore's eyes fell upon first ; it was the wolf the Manitou sent. He wants him to put into the far off hunting ground."

For an instant, only an instant, hope flitted across the face of the doting, and heart broken lover. With the stoicism so natural to these people, they attempted to hide their grief, but too plainly their ill concealed tears betrayed, while they unlocked the almost para-lyzed tongue.

" Did my daughter find her lodge too warm, that she ventured so far away in the dew ? Were her ears closed when her father bid her stay in the shadow of her lodge?"

"The Fawn was sent by Black Snake to meet her father," she replied. "Would Grey Eagle have the Fawn wait for the song of the wish-ton-wish, while the Black Snake sung in her ears; and the Swaying Reed carried her wampum to the chief with the white plume? The Swaying Reed loves Black Snake; and Black Snake sent the Fawn with her wampum, that the eyes of her father and the young chief might fall on her first as they rose the great hill."

Amazement and stupefaction sat for a moment on the features of the Indians during the delivery of this speech. Their swarthy countenances kindled with a fierce expression that told so well the dark thoughts that struggled in their hearts at the perfidy of Black Snake, who had exercised his vengeance in so unmerciful a manner. The threatening tomahawks that filled the air at this convincing proof of his malicious designs, would have terrified any other than that sly, cunning chief. As villians of the present day so often protect themselves with the strong arm of the law intended for their suppression, so Black Snake knowing so well the customs of his people, used their own well meant laws to carry out his sinister plans, and protect himself in so doing. Again amidst the tumult the young chief insisted:

"It was the wolf the chief saw first; 'twas the wolf the Manitou wanted."

So many endorsed the young chief that confusion for the time prevented Great Oak from speaking, which might have been mistaken for yielding; when that crafty chief springing from among the ever-green bushes, confronted the chiefs, and in a loud voice of ferocious exultation and of triumph, tauntingly demanded:

"What says the Sagamore? Does he tell the young warriors a lie? The wolf was in the arms of Black Snake when the Fawn was in the arms of her father."

Turning with an annihilating look upon the base Indian, whose last sentence conveyed an unpardonable taunt to any Indian chief, the Sagamore, with the firmness of the rocks around him and in clear distinct words, replied:

"Dare pass judgement upon the deeds of a sachem who hath sat in council with thy father's father? Look to thyself Black Snake, the hissing spirits in the boiling waters below are calling for thee. I have said."

Bestowing upon his daughter a long look of thwarted love and final resignation, in words at once unyieldingly firm, but full of the Indians' bright hopes and promises for the future, he pronounced her doom, which none dared question.

"My child, the Manitou hath need of thee; thou must soon travel the bright path and join thy mother beyond the clouds. The big moon shows the path brightest now; and that thou mayst not stumble or lose thy way, go prepare thyself at once as the child of thy father should, to joyfully carry the gifts most precious to the Great Manitou for the welfare of thy people. I have said."

The real or pretended indifference to pleasure or pain, one of the great characteristics of the American Indian, even to the joyful manner they would yield, without resistance and evidently without sufficient cause, to torture and death, was owing greatly to the sudden and unalterable decisions of their chiefs, governed by customs formed from their views of a future state, over-ruling all earthly ambitions of these untutored people. Such terrible dooms! The sentence and execution so quickly following each other, and apparently falling upon the poor victim at once, the shock paralyzing their faculties, while pride concealing their softer feelings, transforms them so suddenly into what appears beings indifferent and insensible to the suffering and distress of death and separation or to the expectation of enjoyment and happiness here on earth to themselves or others.

Thus comprehending her inevitable situation and feeling it an honor to be the selected of the Manitou to guide the birchen-bark with precious gifts over the precipice to the happy forest in eternity, where she would meet her long remembered mother, the doomed maiden replied, with tearful smile and subdued voice, "I go my father," and immediately disappeared among the wild vines and bushes that border the banks of Niagara, followed closely by her faithful wolf.

The setting sun that day shed its last rays and warmth upon a busy and sorrowful scene, around thy roaring cataract, Oh, cruel unrelenting fall of waters ! softly painting with mellow light the trees, rocks and thy wild children, unmindful alike, of the sad though customary, preparations for the sacrifice hurriedly pro- ceeding ; the women decking with shells and flowers the fairest. maiden in their tribe, so soon to pass from them forever; the chiefs wrapped in the pride of Indian endurance hide from each other their feelings · no tear betrays, or thoughts even mar the serenity of their countenances, which indicated only submission to fate while the necessary ceremonies were being pro- vided for; and they filled the flower decked bark, moored in the little eddy above the rapids, with highly valuable contributions; and lighted the great pine- fires for the feast and dance, so well furnished and pre- pared by Black Snake, while daylight faded into night, heralded by invisible singers from the surround- ing trees, pouring forth their sleepy monotonous songs, varying only at times in a higher and wilder key, then dying away in the endless roar of the turbu- lent waters around them.

The full moon ascending majestically above the horizon, with its pale, wavering light softened into beauty the rough rocks and banks, revealing the bril- liant and beautiful path that one by one, the wisest and best of their tribe, had followed. Showering its light upon the narrow river path, already filled with the sad hearted maidens leading the submissive Fawn to the waiting boat in the quiet little bay; they hushed the noisy feast with their low sweet voices as they sung her virtues, followed by a subdued and curious crowd of every age and sex. About stepping from the rock to her boat, the Fawn turned to her sire, but e'er she spoke the sachem answered her appealing look.

" I have no word or gift to send by thee, my child. Thou art my all. The Great Oak will soon fall, but in falling must crush his enemies. Thy father will follow thee on the beautiful trail when the Manitou next lights the way," turning, as he finished, his back towards the river, while the Fawn placed herself with mechanical helplessness in the boat. Instantly the unnoticed, but faithful wolf, sprung after her. Arms were stretched to pull him out, but the sachem's voice caused them to fall by the sides of the officious forms to which they belonged.

" The Manitou calls whom he hath use for. If he sent my child through the artfulness of that young chief to the brow of the big hill, he hath also called the wolf, because he hath need of him ; let him go. I have said."

The little bark, held firmly by strong ropes twisted from the inside bark of the elm, and fastened to both ends of the boat and to the side next to the shore, the other ends of the rope held by the weeping maidens who followed the river path, slowly towing the little bark to a point near the brink of the cataract, on the

east border of the river, where a platform of flat rocks whose uneven portions appear here and there above the surface of the water, form a solid foundation to its unsandy shore. There tossing the ropes from them, the light canoe drawn by the powerful current would dance only a moment on the bounding waves, ere it launched into the misty region surrounding the mystical path, where transition is hid from mortal eye. Slowly drawn by the reluctant girls, the Fawn commenced her death song, a simple address to the Manitou, while her thoughts evidently clung to her earthly friends.

> "Thou hath called, Great Manitou, from thy forest on high,
> I come, I'll follow thy ampum-dyed path through the sky;
> Thy gifts hath been poured on the chieftains and braves,
> They send Thee their child on the dark boiling waves;
> Soon in the Beautiful Path she will be,
> Loaded with tears so precious for Thee;
> The grief of my sire, the grief of my brave,
> Oh! Precious the load on this terrible wave;
> But cheered by my chief, as the last leap draws nigh,
> Can I look back and see him from thy Path in the sky?
> One look, O Manitou! 'ere my face turns
> From my father and brave, where my heart still yearns;
> That look; and their tears my offering shall be,
> Oh precious the load I'll carry to Thee,
> As my spirit will rise in the mist o'er the wave,
> While my body floats down to its watery grave."

Suddenly her song was interrupted by another wail, commencing low and gradually rising, till its clear notes seemed to fill the surrounding woods, mingling with the shrieks of the wind as it wound round the

prominent rocks they were slowly approaching. There
on the very rock where the Fawn's little bark would
dart away from the open hands of the sad lamenting
maidens, stood unobserved by all but his own braves,
the tall figure of Grey Eagle, dimly seen through the
suddenly cloudy moonlight, erect against the dark
back ground of the forest, singing in an exulting voice
and manner, words that betrayed his intentions, which
none would dare prevent, or set at naught if accepted
by the Manitou,—a free spontaneous gift of life on his
part, as shown in the words that floated on the night
air to the ears of his hearers.

> "Thou lift'st not thy hand, which only can save
> The dark-eyed maid from thy terrible wave ;
> She is tender and timid, Oh! Great Manitou!
> In the arms of her brave to Thee she must go,
> In the arms of her brave take the terrible flight,
> Together their spirits shall rise into light."

As the ropes fell from the trembling hands of the
towing maidens, the moon in mercy seemed to hide
her face beneath a cloud, veiling in darkness the fear-
ful tragedy, as the Fawn floated off on the pitiless
wave. A splash ; a struggle ; a wild howl, filled the
air, echoing from rock to rock and from shore to shore.
One ray of light from between the clouds revealed the
little boat, as poised an instant in the misty vapor over
the boiling surge, and dark forms gathered on the
rocks from whence the bark had just departed ; while
shout and strife and angry threats grew loud among
the warlike group madly struggling on that brink of

eternity. Great Oak alone could quell the tumult. Followed by some sympathizing chiefs he wound his way among the promiscuous crowd already gathered. On the shore near the brink of the falling waters, on the stony tables extending far out into the water, stood Grey Eagle's warriors, firm as the rocks beneath them. In the center of this group, almost a prisoner of his own braves, was the speechless Grey Eagle ; at his feet crouched the powerful wolf over the prostrate form of the insensible Fawn, alternately howling and licking her face. At the appearance of the old chief clamor ceased, and with difficulty the astonished father was made to understand the cause of the excitement.

At the moment of the Indian girls freeing the boat, the natural instinct of the wolf apprised him of her danger; instantly springing to his loved mistress, fastening his powerful jaws in her deer skin dress, the faithful beast tumbled into the water, struggling with fear and more than common strength to the rock where stood the almost petrified Grey Eagle, who then recognized the omnipotent power that moved to save. Being surrounded by his own braves who quickly and thoughtfully passed them to the shore, re-commenced the pow-wow in which Black Snake's voice was heard above all the others, calling on the Manitou to let his wrath fall on the strangers for robbing him of his gifts, and not on the open hands of his own people, and calling for help to toss them all into the boiling waters, to avert the wrath of the Manitou

THOU hath called, Great Manitou, from thy for-
	est on high,
I come, I'll follow thy wampum-dyed path through
	the sky ;
Thy gifts hath been poured on the chieftans and
	braves,
They send thee their child on the dark boiling
	waves ;
Soon in the beautiful path she will be,
Loaded with tears so precious for Thee ;
The grief of my sire, the grief of my brave,
Oh! Precious the load on this terrible wave ;
But cheered by my chief, as the last leap draws
	nigh,
Can I look back and see him from thy path in the
	sky ?
One look, O Manitou! 'ere my face turns
From my father and brave, where my heart still
	yearns ;
That look ; and their tears my offering shall be,
Oh precious the load I'll carry to Thee,
As my spirit will rise in the mist o'er the wave,
While my body floats down to its watery grave.

www.ingramcontent.com/pod-product-compliance
Lightning Source LLC
Chambersburg PA
CBHW032358020726
47499CB00008B/2805